Logan's Very Strange Day

Logan's Adventure Series: Book 1

Illustrated by: Asia Aurangzeb

Lots of love
from
Mr. Jim and Miss Mary Ann
xx

Logan opened his eyes...

There was a very bright light shining into his room

...making the mirror twinkle

...making Teddy's fur glow

...making the toy cars shine.

He ran to the window.

A huge ball of golden warmth hung in the sky!

...glowing in the garden

...glowing over Dad's fields

....glowing on the cows, the sheep, the pigs, the ponies and the geese.

What a glorious sight!

"Logan! Come on ma brau laddie. Quick as you can, it's a busy day today!"

"Coming Granny."

Logan ran down the stairs, two at a time, remembering all the plans the family had made for the first really warm day of Spring.

Looking for the butterflies in the meadow.

Having a picnic by the lake where they could feed the geese.

Seeing young frogs hopping on the lily pads.

What fun they were going to have!

He could smell Dad's bacon sizzling in the pan...

he didn't want any of that!

He could hear Mum's toast shooting out of the toaster...

he didn't want any of that!

He could see Granny stirring porridge in the pot...

he didn't want any of that!

"Dad! The sun is shining. Are we going to see how many butterflies there are in the meadow?"

"Oh, er, not today ma wee barra! I'm going to have a very busy day!"

"Mum! Can we have a picnic by the lake? And see how many tadpoles have turned into frogs?"

"Er, not today Logan! We're going to be very busy!"

"Granny! Will you come and play on the trampoline with me?"

"Sorry Logan! You'll have to amuse yourself today.

We're all terribly busy!"

Logan sighed and shook his head. Why were they all so busy...but not with him?

He glanced across at Mum and frowned. What was she doing with all his old bibs and Babygro's?

She had taken them out of the cupboard and was laying them out on the sofa at the end of the kitchen. He was far too big for those! Why did she bother keeping them?

Oh well...he would go and find Flora, his best friend, she was always pleased to see him!

She would wag her tail and nuzzle into his chest with her wet, shiny nose, she would look at him with those nut brown eyes as if to say; what great adventures have you got planned today?

Logan slowly made his way to the back door. Nobody tried to stop him, or even suggest he had breakfast before he left.

He plodded down the path, kicking the loose pebbles with the toes of his shoes. Usually Mum told him not to do that 'cos it scuffed the leather. But she wasn't here today...

He opened the gate, which creaked and swung wide on its old rusty hinges. It banged against the fence.
Usually Granny told him to open the gate carefully.
But she wasn't here today...

As he made his way to the kennel where Flora would be waiting, he picked up an empty cola can that someone had thrown over the wall and pretended to drink from it. Usually Dad would've told him not to touch it as it was dirty and had sharp edges. But he wasn't here today...

FLORA

Logan started shouting "Flora! Flora! Here girl!

We're going to have some fun today!"

But Flora wasn't there.

Logan looked inside the kennel.

He looked behind the kennel.

He looked all-round the hedge beside the kennel.

But Flora wasn't there.

Only Mungo, the farm cat, who jumped up and disappeared over the hedge. Suddenly, Logan felt very alone.

Mum, Dad, Granny and now Flora. No one wanted to be with him. Where on earth could Flora be?

The Sheep! Of course! Flora was a sheepdog, so she was probably busy rounding them up and keeping them safe! Feeling a little more cheerful, Logan skipped off down the lane to the field where Dad kept his sheep.

He arrived at the sturdy fence and peered through the wooden stakes. "Flora! Flora!"

"Stop the dreadful shouting, you silly boy!

We are used to peace and quiet round here!"

Logan shot back from the fence and spun round.

Who was talking?

"Flora! Flora!"

"I thought I told you to stop shouting! You aff yer heid?" Logan peered through the fence and came face to face with a rather cross sheep.

"I... I'm sorry! I didn't mean to be rude and disturb you. I was looking for Flora."

"So, I gather. Well she's not here! Although I'd have thought that was perfectly obvious. Have you no eyes?"

"The trouble is, as with all humans, his eyes are both in front, not at the sides like us more advanced creatures!" Logan realised another sheep had wandered over and was joining in.

"You can't see as well as we can, so naturally you'll find it more difficult to discover what it is you're searching for." Logan hadn't thought about this before and began wondering what he would look like if his eyes were where his ears were.

Where would his ears go? At the top of his head?

Gosh, that would make it very difficult to brush your hair!

"So.....are you going to be quiet and leave us alone? Or are you going to stand around looking SHEEPISH all day? Ha-ha!! That was a joke you know! We sheep have a very advanced sense of humour, though not many people know that!"

Logan didn't think he was getting anything useful out of these sheep.

"We can't stand round here chatting all day; they'll be coming to shear us very soon. Phew! It'll be a relief to get rid of all this fleece, it's so hot!"

Logan peered at them with renewed interest. "Is it?" he asked.

"Of course, it is! That's the whole point of wool. You wear it, don't you? Jumpers, scarves, socks, hats? See how good we are to you? And after all our generosity, you come along here bothering our peace and quiet with your ghastly shrieking!"

"I'm really sorry. Honest! But haven't you ANY idea where I can find Flora?"

"Oh, for goodness sake, go and ask the cows!"

Logan thought this was worth trying. In fact, anything was better than having to spend time with these bad-tempered sheep.

He took a deep breath and wandered off to see the cows...hoping and hoping...

Logan arrived at the gate leading to where Reggie's Shetland cows were enjoying the sweet, tasty grass.

Reggie helped Dad run the farm and he always said his cows were like his best friends.

"That must mean they're very kind!" muttered Logan to himself, gazing at their woolly coats, not so thick now that the harsh weather had passed. But their horns looked a little scary! He had a quick look round to see if there was any sign of Flora.

He saw the sun speckled highland hills with their blackthorn and hazel groves.

He saw the hedgerows with their new blossoms smiling up at the sun.

He saw the massive oaks and birches which sheltered the fields from the savage winds in wintery Scotland.

BUT he didn't see Flora...

"I say! Do you have to stare like that? Don't you know it's rude to gape opened-mouthed while we're eating?"

Logan hastily closed his mouth (he hadn't been aware that it was open.)

"Oh...er...I'm very sorry, but I was looking for Flora." Goodness, these cows were as crotchety as the sheep!

"And why look for a dog in a field full of cows? That's very stupid, even for a human! Er... (peering down at Logan) ...you ARE human, aren't you? You're very small."

"Yes, I AM human! And I'm four and a half years old!" Logan felt rather offended at such an insult, and he was most insistent about that "half"!

"Oh well, if you say so!" The cow carried on chomping as if Logan wasn't there. But he persisted.

"Er, excuse me. I really don't want to bother you, but..."

"What! You still here? I thought you'd MOOOVED on by now! Haha! Get it? MOOOVED!!"

Oh dear. Not another animal who thought he was a comedian! But Logan thought he'd better be polite seeing as he wanted his advice.

"I'm sorry! You're awfully funny. Haha! But have you any idea where I could find Flora?"

The cow looked up and sighed.

"Well...have you asked the pigs? They're not particular who they mix with. Although, I never know how anyone could stand that SMELL!! Ugh! Not the kind of creatures WE would ever want to be seen with, but you never know".

"Oh, there's Reggie arriving! Come on ladies, milking time."

All the cows stopped grazing and completely forgot about Logan as they started to make their way to the milking shed.

Logan took a deep breath and wandered off to see the pigs...hoping and hoping...

Even if you didn't know where the pigs were, you just had to follow the smell!

The cow was quite right; it did take a bit of getting used to.

But Logan was getting desperate...

There was an awful lot of chomping and guzzling and gobbling and munching and chewing...

Logan knew that if HE ever made a noise like that at the dinner table he'd be in BIG trouble!

(But it did look like great fun!)

Mind you, he did NOT fancy eating the kind of things they seemed to be enjoying.

The pigs took no notice of him at first. They were all eating from the same trough and they knew if they looked up, another pig would pinch their food.

"Hello! You're new round here. Fancy some grub?"

"Oh...er...no! No thank you! I've already had my breakfast!"

(Actually, he hadn't and he was starting to feel a little peckish, but not for pigswill!!)

"Ohh but I bet your breakfast was nowhere near as good as ours is!" The pig licked a large lump of rotting lettuce leaf from his snout.

"No." mumbled Logan "Nothing at all like this."

A second pig joined in the conversation.

"It's especially delicious today! Strawberry jelly in gravy, with fish heads in yogurt...ohh! And these yummy brussel sprouts covered in custard! You sure you don't want some?"

Logan thought he might well be sick and tore his eyes away from the trough.

"I was actually looking for my best friend Flora.

I can't find her anywhere."

"Oh, Flora hardly ever comes round here, doesn't like it much. You know, she has this really weird taste in food? She just eats meat and chews bones. How boring is that! I, being an expert in food, once suggested she dipped her meat in rice pudding with curry sauce, but she didn't seem to like that idea!"

Logan smiled as he thought of all the fun times with Flora. "Actually her favourite food is sausages."

The pigs stopped chomping and stared at Logan.

Their little piggy eyes squinted at him and their snouts twitched at him in a rather worrying way.

"Sausages? Not....PORK sausages by any chance...?"

Logan immediately understood their concern and hastened to reassure them.

"No! Beef! Not Pork!! Definitely not pork, only beef.

She won't touch pork!"

The pigs relaxed a little.

Logan began to think about these big, fat guzzling creatures and remembered how much he loved bacon...and ham...and gammon....and roast pork. He did feel a little guilty, but he was also a little hungry.

"I...er...I'd better go now. Have you any idea where Flora might have gone?"

"Try the ponies. They know everything"

It was fascinating how they could manage to speak without lifting their heads from the trough.

Logan took a deep breath and wandered off to see the ponies... hoping and hoping....

He loved visiting Dad's Highland ponies.

They were such beautiful animals and very useful.

Dad always said people used to visit the farm and hire them for Pony Trekking and this money came in very handy when there were bills to pay.

(Although Logan was not really sure why they had to pay Uncle Bill.)

But then, grownups said LOTS of things he didn't understand.

He arrived at the field where the ponies were taking their exercise. They still had their thick winter coats, but they'd be shedding them and be sleek and slim for the warm weather.

"Well look who's come visiting! Good morning young Logan. What are you doing all on your own?"

"I'm looking for Flora, I can't find her anywhere"

Hector, the pony who had spoken, shook his long untrimmed mane as he came closer to the fence.

"Actually, laddie, I haven't seen Flora myself for a day or two. Wonder where she can be? Have you asked the other animals?

"Yes, apart from the geese. Nobody has seen Flora!"

“Here, do you fancy a ride while you're here?

We could have a wee gallop around the field?”

Logan looked up at Hector. He wasn't all that large as horses go, but he towered above a four and a half year old and it made him a little nervous.

"I don't think I've got the time for that, er, thanking you very much. Maybe another time when Dad's with me."

Hector chuckled and cantered off..."Nae bother laddie, nae bother!"

Logan took a deep breath and wondered off to see the geese...hoping and hoping...

It was always so peaceful down by the lake. Strictly speaking Logan wasn't allowed to come down here on his own in case he got too close to the water's edge and fell in.

Flora used to bark whenever he got curious and stepped too near to where the thick water reeds grew. But he'd have to manage by himself today as Flora wasn't here.

The geese, as always, were gliding so elegantly along the surface of the lake, hardly making a ripple.

This always seemed like magic to Logan.

Whenever HE went for a paddle, he caused huge splashes and then he'd lose his balance and fall in the water. And it didn't taste very nice. Yuk!

"Excuse me."

The geese turned their heads slowly and majestically and stared at him.

"Did you want something little boy?"

"I was wondering if you'd seen Flora, my sheepdog, as you were gliding by?"

"A dog! Oh, dear no! Big, untidy, messy creatures.

No style...no dignity...no class", replied the geese.

They made their way across the lake and Logan wondered what he was going to do next. There really was nothing else for it; he'd have to go home.

He took a deep breath and set off for home, and then he heard a familiar voice.

"Well, hello young Logan. And what are you doing all on your own so far from the house?"

It was Reggie the farmhand! He wandered over to Logan and picked him up, sitting him astride his huge shoulders.

Logan loved Reggie, who always had toffees in his pocket and always had time to chat.

"Everybody is too busy for me today, Reggie. They've all got more important things to do. Even Flora's disappeared."

"Flora! Has nobody told you? Aw, come on laddie. I can take you to Flora alright!" He chuckled. "Have you got a lovely surprise waiting for you!"

Reggie carried Logan until they came to the old barn behind the farmhouse. Then he lowered him down and told him to look inside. Logan ran off into the barn. It took him a while for his eyes to get used to the dimness of the inside.

Then he heard scuffling, yelping noises coming from the corner where there were some old sacks and straw forming a kind of bed.

And there was Flora...with six tiny and absolutely adorable puppies!

So, this was why Logan couldn't find her. He turned to Reggie.

"Can we keep them? The puppies, please can we keep them?"

"Ah, well laddie, you'll need to ask your Dad that and I think he may just have more important things on his mind at the moment!"

Logan climbed carefully over the squirming pups to give Flora a hug.

She gave his face a warm lick with a big wet tongue as if to say... "Where have you been all morning? I've been waiting for you."

Logan at last tore himself away from Flora and the pups and ran into the kitchen.

Granny was there on her own taking a fresh batch of loaves out of the Aga.

"Ah, there you are Logan! You missed breakfast this morning; fancy a slice of bread with strawberry jam?"

"Granny! Flora's had pups! Can we keep them?"

"One thing at a time laddie. Here's your bread and jam, and you'll need to speak to your Dad about the puppies."

Logan took a large bite of the warm bread, he was starving!

"Where is Dad? And Mum?"

Granny sat beside him. "Well Logan, while you were out playing, Dad had to take Mum to the hospital".

Logan looked up in alarm, strawberry jam trickling down his chin....

"Hospital Granny?"

"Now dinna fash yersel Logan; you have a new baby brother. Dad will be back shortly to take you to meet him!"

Logan stared at her in amazement, the strawberry jam now forming stripes down his t-shirt.

Suddenly everybody's strange behaviour became clear.

Suddenly life made sense again.

In fact...life was going to be better than ever!

The perfect ending ...

to a VERY strange day!

For More Information about my Other Books in the Series:

Logan's Adventure Stories

Please visit:

Facebook: www.facebook.com/logansadventurestories

Instagram: www.instagram.com/logansadventurestories

Website: www.logansadventurestories.com

Printed in Great Britain
by Amazon